J

Magdalen Nabb

Josie Smith
in Autumn

Illustrations by Karen Donnelly

Collins

An imprint of HarperCollins*Publishers*

First published in Great Britain by Collins in 2000
Collins is an imprint of HarperCollins*Publishers* Ltd
77-85 Fulham Palace Road, Hammersmith,
London W6 8JB

1 3 5 7 9 8 6 4 2

ISBN 0 00 675410 4

The HarperCollins website address is
www.**fire**and**water**.com

Printed and bound in Great Britain by
Caledonian International Book Manufacturing Ltd,
Glasgow G64

CONTENTS

JOSIE SMITH AND FRIENDS

Josie Smith

Ginger

Mum

Gran

Eileen

Geoffrey Taylor

Gary Grimes

Jimmy Earnshaw

Rawley Baxter

Rawley's sister

Miss Potts

Mr Scowcroft

Mr Kefford

Mrs Chadwick

Ann Lomax

Tahara

JOSIE SMITH'S
BLACKBERRY PIE

Josie Smith opened the front door and went out on the doorstep to sniff the day.

'Morning, Josie,' said Mrs Chadwick, sweeping the step of her corner shop on the other side of the street.

'Morning, Mrs Chadwick,' said Josie Smith. Then she looked up at the sky. The strip between the two rows of black roofs and chimneys was deep blue with no clouds and the

morning was fresh and warm. The milk van
with its rattling crates was still down the street
because it was Saturday and Mrs Holt had to
knock at everybody's door for the milk money.

'Put your cardigan on!' shouted Josie's mum.

'My arms are not cold!' shouted Josie Smith.
'It's sunshining!'

'Josie! I'll not tell you again!'

Josie Smith went back inside. Her mum was in the front room and there was a boring smell of polish and dusters.

'Don't you go out without your cardigan.'

'Aw, Mum!' said Josie Smith, but her mum was plugging the Hoover in and didn't answer.

'Can I put my new navy blue one on, then?' asked Josie Smith.

'That's for when you go back to school,' said Josie's mum, 'now mind out of the way.'

'Just for today,' said Josie Smith, 'and then I'll save it for school. Go on, Mum, can I? Mum, you're hoovering my feet.'

'Well, mind out of the way. Will you, for goodness' sake, get that cardigan on and go out to play.'

Josie Smith went upstairs and opened the drawer where her new cardigan was folded all smooth and flat. It smelled of all the new clothes in tissue paper and white boxes in the warm little shop near the post office.

'My mum didn't say no,' whispered Josie Smith to Percy Panda on the bed, 'she only said I had to put my cardigan on.'

Josie Smith put her new cardigan on and buttoned it up so carefully that there was only one buttonhole left over at the bottom. Sometimes, if she wasn't careful, there were two. Then she ran downstairs and out the back door as fast as her wellingtons would go.

'I'm playing out!' she shouted as she banged the back yard gate. But her mum was hoovering and didn't hear.

When she went next door to call for Eileen, Eileen stuck her tongue out and said, 'I'm not playing with you because I've got a new doll and you haven't to touch it.'

'Why haven't I?' asked Josie Smith. She hated dolls like that, anyway, because they were thin and spiky but she liked the fancy clothes and handbags and the pink plastic high-heeled shoes that Eileen had spread round her on the rug.

'Because my mum said only I have to play with it.'

'You're supposed to let me play with it as well because I'm your best friend and I let you play with my toys.'

'You haven't got any toys,' Eileen said. 'All

you've got is a rubbishy old doll and a stupid panda.'

'Percy's not stupid!' shouted Josie Smith, 'You are!'

Eileen stuck her tongue out again and Josie Smith went out of Eileen's front door, stamping her wellies hard.

She hopped down the street for a bit, singing, 'If you tread on a nick you'll marry a stick and a blackjack'll come to your wedding.' Josie Smith never trod on nicks.

When she got to Gary Grimes's house, Gary Grimes was standing on his doorstep going Vrumm Vrumm Vrumm with a toy car.

'We can play Cowies and Indians, if you want,' Gary Grimes said.

'I'm not,' Josie Smith said, 'because I always have to be tied to the lamppost.'

'We can play wrestling, then,' Gary Grimes said.

Josie Smith was just going to push him over and start when she remembered her new cardigan and said, 'I can't.'

Gary Grimes went in and shut the door.

'If you tread on a nick you'll marry a stick and a blackjack'll come to your wedding.'

Josie Smith skipped on down the street until she came to Jimmy Earnshaw's house and knocked on his door. Josie Smith liked Jimmy Earnshaw. He gave Josie Smith her ginger cat and sometimes he let her ride on the crossbar of his two wheeler and he was her friend even though he was nearly eleven. Josie Smith was going to marry him when she grew up. But Mrs Earnshaw opened the door and said, 'He's not in, love. He's gone off somewhere on his bike.' And she smiled at Josie Smith and shut the door.

Rawley Baxter came running up the street with his anorak tied round his neck, yelling,

'Derda derda derda derda, derda derda derda derda, Batman!'

When he got to Josie Smith he stopped, out of breath, and said, 'I'm going to call for Jimmy Earnshaw.'

'No, you're not,' Josie Smith said, 'because he's gone out somewhere really important on his bike. His mum said. And anyway, you're not big enough to play with him.'

'D'you want to play Batman?'

'No,' said Josie Smith, 'I'm not being stupid Robin. Where's your sister?'

Rawley Baxter's little sister never got fed up of being Robin and running round after Rawley Baxter all day, even though he ran too fast for her and she always fell.

'She's not so well and she can't play out. Are you coming or not?'

He didn't even wait for Josie Smith to say

14

no, he just went on running up the street and shouting at Robin to get in the Batmobile. He didn't really care whether there was anybody running behind him or not.

Josie Smith skipped down the street until she got to her gran's. Her gran was in the front room and there was a boring smell of polish and dusters.

'Gran?'

'Hello, love. Are you not playing out? It's a lovely morning.'

'There's nobody playing,' said Josie Smith. 'Can I go in the big drawer?'

The big drawer was full of things that Josie Smith could play with. There were some old wooden skittles and a paintbox and annuals with the edges of their covers worn away to grey fluff.

'You'll have to wait a while,' said Josie's gran, 'because I'm going to polish the sideboard.'

Josie Smith sat down on the rug and grumbled, 'I'm fed up.'

'Come here a minute,' said Josie's gran, 'and I'll tell you a little secret.'

Josie Smith liked secrets so she went up to her gran and listened.

'Don't tell anybody else,' whispered Josie's gran, 'but today's my birthday. I bet you can't guess how old I am.'

Josie Smith thought a bit. Her gran must be very very old. She couldn't see as well as she used to and she didn't like running.

'Are you thirty?' asked Josie Smith. That was the oldest she could think of.

'I'm a little bit older than that,' said Josie's gran. 'I'm thinking of having a birthday party, too. D'you want to come?'

'A real party? With balloons?' asked Josie Smith.

'I don't see why not,' said Josie's gran, 'There'll probably be a balloon or two in the big drawer if we look.'

Then Josie Smith thought hard and said, 'I can't come to your party, Gran, because I haven't got a present for you.'

'Well that's a shame,' said Josie's gran, 'I'd have liked you to come. Oh well, never mind. I'll invite Mrs Chadwick. She has all sorts in her shop so she'll bring me a present, won't she? She might even bring me a cake.'

'She's got liquorice torpedos, as well,' said Josie Smith, 'and red Spanish.'

There was a big lump coming in Josie Smith's

throat to make her cry because she wanted to come to Gran's party.

'I don't know if I fancy liquorice torpedos,' said Josie's gran. 'Some black and white mints would be nice. But d'you know what I'd really like? I went up to Mr Kefford's this morning for a pound of onions and lettuce and some beetroot and he had some lovely blackberries and I thought to myself, a blackberry pie, that would be nice.'

'And did you buy some?' asked Josie Smith.

'Well, to tell you the truth, I hadn't much money in my purse and I wondered if there were still blackberries growing in the lane at the back of Mr Scowcroft's allotment. I always picked blackberries there when I was a girl. If I made some pastry and you went to pick a few blackberries for me we could have a pie at my birthday party. What d'you think?'

'Would it count as a present?' asked Josie Smith.

'It would be the best present in the world,' said Josie's gran. 'Better even than black and white mints. Of course, it'd be hard work, picking blackberries.'

'I don't care,' said Josie Smith.

'And hot, as well, standing in one place with the sun on your head.'

'I don't care,' said Josie Smith.

'And you're bound to get your hands and legs scratched.'

'I don't care.'

'And blackberry juice all down your frock.'

'I don't care.'

'We'd better look for the basket, then.'

They found the basket in the cubby hole where Josie Smith played hiding. There was an old fur coat there with fur that came out in lumps if you pulled and there was a smell of old shoes and mothballs. The blackberrying basket was small and very dusty. Josie's gran gave it a bit of a wash and put a paper towel in it to cover a hole.

'You ought to have a sunbonnet on,' said Josie's gran.

'What's a sunbonnet?' asked Josie Smith.

'We'll have another look in the cubby hole. You'll have to crawl right to the back to the shelf where the hatboxes are. Round boxes. Get the dark green one.'

Josie Smith crawled out with the big round box and Gran took the lid off.

'Choose,' said Josie's gran.

There was a white organza bonnet with a frill round your face and Josie Smith tried it on but she looked like somebody in a nursery rhyme.

'What do you think?' said Josie's gran.

'Is it a dressing-up hat?' asked Josie Smith.

'I think it had better be,' said Josie's gran. 'If we gave you a watering can you'd look like Mary, Mary, Quite Contrary. No, that won't do for blackberrying. Try this. My Breton straw hat. I did love it. And it's dark blue, the colour of blackberries, with elastic in case it falls off. There.'

Josie Smith looked at herself in the mirror over the dresser and smiled.

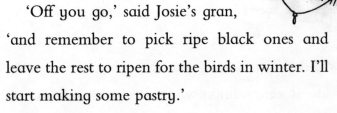

'Off you go,' said Josie's gran, 'and remember to pick ripe black ones and leave the rest to ripen for the birds in winter. I'll start making some pastry.'

'If you tread on a nick you'll marry a stick and a blackjack'll come to your wedding.'

Josie Smith, not treading on nicks, walked carefully up the street with her basket. Batman Rawley Baxter came flying down with his anorak wings and nearly crashed into her.

'Where are you going in that stupid hat?'

'Blackberrying,' said Josie Smith, 'you can't come because you've got to have a hat and a basket like this.'

Rawley Baxter dashed in his house and Josie Smith walked on. Then she heard him shouting: 'Hey! Wait for me!'

Rawley Baxter was following her wearing his Batman hood with ears and carrying a plastic supermarket bag.

Gary Grimes was on his doorstep going Vrumm Vrumm Vrumm with a toy car.

'Where are you going in that stupid hat?' he said.

'Blackberrying,' said Josie Smith, 'and you

can't come because you've got to have a hat and a basket like this.'

'Rawley Baxter's only got his Batman hat and a plastic carrier,' said Gary Grimes. He dashed inside his house and Josie Smith walked on with Rawley Baxter following. Then they heard Gary Grimes shouting, 'Hey! Wait for me!'

Gary Grimes was following them up the street wearing a knitted bob hat and carrying a plastic box from the fridge.

Eileen was on her doorstep talking to her doll.

'Where are you going in that stupid hat?' Eileen said.

'Blackberrying,' said Josie Smith, 'and this is a special blackberrying hat, the same colour as blackberries, and this is a special basket and you can't come.'

Eileen dashed inside her house and Josie Smith walked on with Rawley Baxter and Gary Grimes following. Then they heard Eileen shouting, 'Hey! Wait for me!'

Eileen was following them up the street wearing the straw bonnet of her Little Bo-Peep costume that she got for the fancy-dress party and carrying the basket that had held her flowers when she was a bridesmaid.

When Josie Smith turned round and saw her, she wished for a minute she'd chosen the

Mary, Mary hat with the big frill. Then she remembered that her hat was the colour of blackberries. She felt its brim and smiled and went on up the street followed by Rawley Baxter and Gary Grimes and Eileen.

They reached the top of their street and turned the corner to go up towards their school and Mr Scowcroft's allotment. When they passed the corner of Albert Street all the children playing out there started to shout.

'Look at Josie Smith with a lid on!'

'Look at soppy Eileen!'

'And what's Grimesy supposed to be?'

They knew what Rawley Baxter was supposed to be because he was always Batman.

Then somebody shouted, 'It's a fancy-dress party!' And all the children from Albert Street started following Josie Smith.

'It's not fancy dress!' shouted Josie Smith. 'It's blackberrying and you can't all come because there won't be enough and we have to leave some for the birds and, anyway, you've got to have a hat and a basket like this!'

But nobody could hear. Josie Smith turned right at the dirt track that went behind Mr Scowcroft's allotment, followed by Rawley Baxter and Gary Grimes and Eileen and all the children from Albert Street. Mr Scowcroft's hens were scratching for worms behind the chicken wire fence but they looked up and ran away on their stiff legs, clucking with fright.

'I'm sorry,' Josie Smith said, because the hens were her friends and she sometimes helped to feed them. 'Don't be frightened. I won't let anybody touch you.'

But when they had run a few steps, the hens forgot and started scratching for worms again.

When she reached the blackberry bushes, Josie Smith remembered her cardigan and thought hard. Her cardigan, like the straw hat, was as dark blue as the blackberries so it wouldn't matter so much if it got stained. Then she had another think and remembered the scratchy brambles. She took off her cardigan and folded it up nicely so it would look as good as new and put it down carefully on some clean grass. Then she started picking, choosing big shiny blackberries the exact colour of her hat. Rawley Baxter picked one sour red one, put it in his mouth, spat it out and ran off along the dirt track being Batman. Gary Grimes copied

27

Josie Smith, picking where she picked and getting in her way. Eileen tried to pick a blackberry but she scratched her hand and ran home crying with her Bo-Peep hat and her bridesmaid's basket. The children from Albert Street watched Josie Smith and then started picking blackberries for themselves. None of them had bags or baskets so they put them in their pockets or ate them or threw them at each other. Josie Smith got mad at them because they were wasting blackberries but she couldn't fight them all so she shouted, 'You've got to leave some for the birds!'

'You've got to leave some for the birds!' whined a big boy, imitating her.

'Don't be so soft!' another one said and thwacked a bramble at her, scratching her arm. Another one knocked her hat off but it stayed on her back because of the elastic. Gary Grimes dropped his plastic box and ran away.

Josie Smith's chest was going Bam Bam Bam because now she was all by herself with the children from Albert Street. She kept on picking blackberries, not looking at any of them until one of the big boys shouted, 'Let's go on the swings!'

They all ran off, shouting and pushing.

'You can't port up for toffee!'

'I can! I can go over the bumps!'

'Can you heck!'

'I can!'

Then they were gone.

It was very quiet. The sun was hot on Josie Smith's fringe and she put her hat back on. Trickles of blackberry juice ran down her arms as she reached for the ripe fruit high on the bush. The juice stung her scratches and the work made her thirsty and the reaching made her arms ache but she only thought about choosing the warm shiny berries and collecting enough for a pie. When all the berries she could reach on the first bush were red, she moved to the next one. She heard some birds chattering and chirping but she didn't see them.

'I'm leaving all the red ones,' she promised them, 'and there are loads of fat black ones too high up for me to reach so you don't need to worry.'

The birds chirped and chattered, the sun warmed the berries and Josie Smith moved slowly down the lane, choosing and picking, scratching her arms and legs and filling her basket. When her arms wouldn't reach up any more she sat down on a grassy clump between the bushes and had a little rest. She tried one or two of the blackberries to make sure they were soft and sweet but not so many because they were her gran's present. Then she carried on picking.

When she reached the bottom of the lane there was a stone wall and no more bushes. Josie Smith looked in her basket. She thought the pile of blackberries looked enough for a pie. Then she sniffed. There was a good smell coming from somewhere. A smell of dinner, all kinds of dinner. Chops and mint sauce, sausage and chips, roast chicken and stuffing, meat and potato pie. And it was all coming from over the stone wall. It wasn't as high as Josie Smith, so she put her basket of blackberries on it and scrambled up to look over. On the other side was a back lane and washing and gates into

people's back yards. The dinner smells were coming from all the kitchens in the row. It was dinner time! Josie Smith's chest went Bam Bam Bam. She was late for her dinner! Her mum would be shouting for her in the street and when she saw her come running home she'd see she was wearing her new... her new cardigan!

Josie Smith dropped down from the wall, scraping her knees as she went, and stood there in a panic looking at her bare arms streaked with blackberry juice. Her new cardigan! Where was it? Where? Josie Smith ran up the dirt lane, crying with fear. She couldn't go home without it but she couldn't think where to look. Had she put it down to climb the wall?

She ran back down the lane crying but it wasn't there. Had she put it down when she stopped for a rest? She ran back up the lane crying but she couldn't remember where she'd stopped and she couldn't see the cardigan anywhere. What if one of the children from Albert Street had pinched it? She ran to the top of the lane, to the first bush where the children from Albert Street had been. But what was the use of that if they'd pinched it? Josie Smith stood there, not knowing where to run next but knowing she'd get smacked if she went home.

Then she saw it, lying neatly folded on a patch of clean grass, just where she'd left it.

Josie Smith rubbed her eyes on her

blackberry-stained arm and the salty tears stung her scratches but she didn't care. She put her cardigan on and buttoned it up carefully but her hands were shaky from crying and this time there were two buttonholes left over. There was no time to try again because it was dinner time and she still had to run all the way down to her gran's.

Josie Smith started running as fast as her wellingtons would go, past Mr Scowcroft's allotment, past the corner of Albert Street and all the way down her own street to her gran's.

'Hello, love,' said her gran. 'I've got some good news for you. There were no balloons left in the big drawer but I looked in my magic handbag and, would you believe it, there was a full packet! So my party will be a real party. You can bring Eileen as well, if you want to. Now then, I'd better get my blackberry pie made. Josie? Josie! Whatever's to do with you?'

All the way to Gran's house, Josie Smith had been running fast and thinking about the safe warm feel of her arms in the new cardigan that wasn't lost. She hadn't thought about anything else and she didn't notice that she wasn't carrying her basket any more. Her gran's basket. Her gran's birthday blackberries.

'Come on,' said Josie's gran, 'let's be having you. Come in the kitchen. The pastry's already rolled out so we'll be done in five minutes. Your mum's just gone home and your dinner will be ready soon.'

'Gran,' whispered Josie Smith, 'have you got any blackberries in your magic handbag?'

But Gran didn't hear her. She didn't always hear all the things you said to her.

35

She didn't see as well as she used to, either, so when she got a flannel and washed the blackberry juice tears from Josie Smith's cheeks, she thought they were just blackberry juice and didn't notice there were some more tears ready to spill over.

'If I give you the colander,' Josie's gran said, 'will you wash the blackberries while I line the plate?'

Josie Smith took the colander and didn't say anything.

'Get on, then,' said Josie's gran. 'The basket of blackberries is there in the sink. Try not to splash.'

Josie Smith washed the blackberries, trying not to splash.

'It's a funny thing,' said Josie's gran, 'but I thought after you'd gone I should have told you to leave your full basket on the wall outside the back gate when you got to the bottom of the lane. I always had to and your mum did, too. And do you know why?'

'No,' said Josie Smith in a very small voice.

'Because if we walked all the way back up and came round the street way what do you think would have happened?'

'Was the basket too heavy?' asked Josie Smith.

'No, it wasn't! It was too light because, by the time we'd walked all that way with it, hot and thirsty and tired, we'd have eaten every single blackberry. So we'd leave the basket on the wall and my mother would come out at the back gate and get it. Just fancy, you thought of it by yourself. When I spotted the basket from the kitchen window it took me back years to when your mum was a little girl. Have you done?'

'Yes,' said Josie Smith and they poured the shiny blackberries into their pastry bed and sprinkled them with sugar and covered them up.

And when they had trimmed the edges, Josie Smith made the trimmings of pastry into twirly writing. There wasn't enough to write Happy Birthday so she just wrote one word: Gran.

When Josie Smith went home she was carrying the blackberrying basket which her gran had given to her to keep. In the basket, carefully folded by Gran, was her new cardigan, lying between two squares of paper towel to keep it from blackberry stains.

'Are you sure you don't want to put it on?'

'I'm hot with running,' said Josie Smith, 'and I might be a bit dirty with blackberrying and it's new and I shouldn't really wear it and my mum might shout.'

Her mum shouted.

'What did I tell you about going out without a cardigan?'

'I didn't go out without it,' said Josie Smith, 'I took it off when I got hot.'

'If you've lost another cardigan I'll...'

'I haven't lost it,' said Josie Smith, 'it's in this basket that Gran gave me.' And she went up and put it away.

Gran had a good birthday party with balloons, Josie Smith and Josie's mum, and Eileen and Mrs Chadwick. Mrs Chadwick brought Gran some black and white mints and some liquorice torpedos for Josie Smith and Eileen. But then they started having another cup of tea and another and another and talking so Josie Smith and Eileen went out the back to play.

When they were out, Josie Smith looked hard at the wall on the other side of the back street. It was very high on this side so that only grownups could reach the top of it and Josie Smith couldn't tell if the blackberry lane was really on the other side. She thought she'd ask her mum about it when they got home but she forgot.

Gran had given Josie's mum another two pieces of pie to take home and they ate them next day with rice pudding after their Sunday dinner.

Josie's mum said, 'I think this is the best blackberry pie I ever tasted. When it comes to pastry your gran has a magic touch.'

'And she's got a magic handbag as well,' said Josie Smith, 'and my blackberrying basket's magic.'

'You are a comic,' said Josie's mum. 'Now, eat your rice pudding as well.'

'I am,' said Josie Smith, 'and my basket is magic and I'm going to keep it for ever and ever.'

'You know you always lose things,' said Josie's mum.

'I won't lose my basket,' said Josie Smith, 'because it's magic and it knows its way home.'

JOSIE SMITH AND THE
TOOTH FAIRY

Eileen rattled the letter box and shouted through, 'Is she ready?'

'It's Eileen!' shouted Josie Smith. 'Mum! I'm going to be late!'

'You're not late,' said Josie's mum. 'Finish your breakfast.'

'I can't or I'll really be late!'

'Well, clean your teeth, then. Where's your ribbon?'

Josie Smith dashed upstairs. She pretended to clean her teeth, wiggling the brush about without any toothpaste. Then she wiggled a tooth that was a bit loose. She looked at herself in the bathroom mirror and smiled, smoothing her thick short fringe that her mum had cut last night. Then she dashed down again. Eileen rattled the letter box. Josie Smith dashed upstairs and found her ribbon and dashed downstairs for her mum to tie it. Eileen rattled the letter box. Josie Smith dashed upstairs to say goodbye to Percy and whisper in his ear, 'I'm going back to school today and I like my fringe and I've got my new cardigan on and I'll be having a new teacher and a new pencil as well.' Then she dashed down again and put her coat on. Eileen rattled the letter box. Mum put an apple in Josie's pocket for playtime and Josie Smith set off.

Ginger was sitting on the doorstep washing

his whiskers when Josie Smith opened the door. Josie Smith bent down to stroke him and Eileen said, 'Come on.' Then she said, 'Who's cut your hair?'

'My mum,' said Josie Smith.

'I always go to the hairdresser's,' Eileen said.

'I don't care,' said Josie Smith, smoothing her fringe and smiling.

'That's a pudding basin haircut,' Eileen said.

'It is not,' said Josie Smith. She didn't really know what it meant but it sounded horrible.

'Oh yes it is,' said Eileen, 'and I've got two new slides and a new satchel, so ner ner ner!'

Josie Smith looked at the hairslides in Eileen's blonde curly hair. They were little pink wooden dolls with yellow curls like Eileen's and red spots on their frocks. Eileen's satchel was pink and yellow, too.

'I don't care,' said Josie Smith but she said it with her eyes shut because it was a lie. 'What have you got in it, anyway?'

'A packet of crisps,' said Eileen, 'and a cream bun from Mrs Chadwick's and a bar of chocolate and a big new packet of felt-tip pens and a comic.'

Josie Smith felt the smooth shiny apple in her pocket. She didn't say anything. When they got to Mr Scowcroft's allotment, just before their school, they saw Mr Scowcroft feeding his hens. There were some lettuces in a row and some pom pom dahlias at the back near the wire fence. Josie Smith liked pom pom dahlias, especially the bright red ones. She liked the hens as well and she wished she could stay and help Mr Scowcroft feed them like she did in the holidays. But today she had to go back to school with no new hairslides, no new satchel, no crisps and cake and chocolate and no new felt-tip pens. She felt her fringe but it didn't make her smile any more. What was a pudding basin haircut?

The sun was shining and the morning was fresh and smelled of leaves and bacon sandwiches. Up at school, the boys were playing football in the yard and shouting.

'Give it here, Grimesy!'

'Over here! Over here!'

'That's a foul, that is!'

'Give us that ball back or I'll bash you!'

Josie Smith and Eileen stayed at the other end of the yard, walking by the railings with their arms round each other.

'D'you want to know something?' Eileen said, 'Only, you haven't to tell anybody else.'

'I won't tell,' said Josie Smith.

Eileen whispered in her ear, 'We're not

going to let Gary Grimes and
Rawley Baxter sit at our table in
the new class.'

'How can we stop them?'
asked Josie Smith. 'We were put
at our tables in the new class
before we broke up for the
summer holidays.'

'Well, it doesn't matter
because our teacher's new and
she won't know who we are or
where we're supposed to sit. So,
listen: I get right at the front
when we line up and Ann
Lomax and Tahara as well and
we dash in and get a table
together. You stand at the back
of the line and when we go in
you go to Ann Lomax's place
and Gary Grimes'll follow you

and Rawley Baxter'll follow him. Then you get up and come and sit with us.'

Josie Smith liked Tahara but she didn't like Ann Lomax so much and none of them could do sums so there wouldn't be anybody to help her.

'I'd rather have Geoffrey Taylor,' Josie Smith said, 'instead of Ann Lomax.'

'Just because you want to marry him,' Eileen said.

'I do not want to marry him. I'm marrying Jimmy Earnshaw because he's big and he gave me Ginger and he's got a two-wheeler. And, anyway, I'll have to help everybody with their reading and nobody'll help me with my sums.'

'Who cares about sums?' Eileen said. 'Ann Lomax has got two new bangles and she's going to let me wear one all day.'

'How do you know?'

Eileen got the packet of crisps out of her

satchel and opened it. 'I saw her on Saturday, shopping with her mum, and she promised and, anyway, Rawley Baxter and Gary Grimes can't read or do sums.'

'Geoffrey Taylor can,' said Josie Smith watching Eileen eat her crisps and wishing she'd finished her breakfast.

'I don't care and he's not sitting with us because he said I was soft and he's got horrible ginger hair!' Eileen ran off and started walking round the playground with her arm round Ann Lomax, whispering secrets and giving her a crisp.

Josie Smith waited by herself near the railings for the whistle. She felt hungry. When the whistle blew she ran as fast as she could to her line. Ann Lomax and Eileen got there first and Josie Smith stood right at the back. She didn't see Tahara. The whistle blew again and everybody was quiet and they walked in.

They went to their new classroom. There was a little corridor where you went in, with hooks for their coats and a bench with cages underneath for their gym shoes. Somebody had stuck names under each hook. Everybody was pushing and shoving to find their names except Gary Grimes and Rawley Baxter who couldn't read and always dumped their coats on the bench. Josie Smith, the last in the line, was worrying. If their teacher was new, how did she know all their names to stick them on the hooks? Did she know them all? Eileen's coat and satchel and Ann Lomax's coat and satchel were hung up so their names must be there. Had their mums been to school to say? Their mums were always coming to school. Josie Smith, worrying hard, burrowed behind the coats as the new teacher said, 'Bring a chair all of you, and come and sit round me. Any chair will do.'

Josie Smith, still worrying and still burrowing, heard her say, 'What are you doing over there?'

Josie Smith, still worrying, stopped burrowing and stood still. Her chest was going Bam Bam Bam.

'I can't find my name,' she said in a tiny voice.

'You'll have to speak up if you want me to hear you,' the new teacher said. 'Now, come and sit down. Just hang your coat on any free hook if you can't see yours. Hurry up.'

Josie Smith hurried up but she didn't like hanging her coat on Gary Grimes's hook. Once he'd pinched her gym shoes when he couldn't find his own. He might pinch her camouflage green anorak and then she'd get shouted at.

When everybody was sitting down, the new teacher said, 'Good morning, children.'

'Good mor-ning-Miss...' Then they were stuck.

'I'm Miss Taylor,' the new teacher said.

Josie Smith stared hard at Miss Taylor. She had nice lipstick and she smiled. She had dark hair, nearly black, and a haircut just like Josie Smith's. She called the register and Josie Smith spoke up when it was her turn and then the bell went for assembly.

When her class marched in, Mrs Ormerod was playing the piano very hard with wobbly arms and the baby class and Infant One were already lined up at the front. When everybody was in the hall, Miss Potts, the headmistress, marched in, banging her heels, and climbed up the steps to the stage. Mr Bannister, the caretaker, came in, too, and stood at the side with his brush and a horrible look on his face like he did when somebody was sick on his newly-polished floor. Nobody had been sick. Not yet.

They sang *All Things Bright and Beautiful* and said their prayers and sang *I Love the Sun*.

Then everything went quiet and Mr Bannister came on the stage and stood next to Miss Potts.

'Now then!' roared Miss Potts, 'Mr Bannister is here with me for a very good reason. He's been in my office this morning and told me that he has had to sweep the whole playground before assembly. Isn't that right, Mr Bannister?'

Mr Bannister opened his mouth to speak and then shut it again because Miss Potts was still talking. Her face was getting redder.

'That whole playground was littered with toffee papers and crisp packets and the like before school even started and, if I know anything, it'll be the same after morning playtime, dinner time and afternoon playtime. Well, it's going to stop! I will not have litter in my school! I don't know what your parents are thinking about, sending you to school with all that rubbish that will rot your teeth and spoil your appetites. There's a good dinner provided for you that your parents pay for and if they haven't the sense to see that you eat properly, I have! Hands up all those who've brought sweet stuff and crisps and the like to school today?'

Nearly all the hands went up. Miss Potts's face went so red it was nearly purple. 'Right! You give all that stuff to your class teacher and she'll give it back to you at home time. Is that understood? I said, is that understood!'

'Yes-Miss-Potts,' said everybody.

'You! Josie Smith! I didn't see your hand go up. What have you brought?'

'An apple,' said Josie Smith in a small and frightened voice, wondering if she were going to get shouted at.

'An apple! I should think so, too! From now on you all bring an apple to school or nothing and the cores go in the bin that's out there in the yard. And if I catch anybody... anybody... throwing crisp papers around, or toffee papers, I'll have your parents in! Is that understood?'

'Yes-Miss-Potts.'

'Well, see that it is. Thank you, Mrs Ormerod.'

Mrs Ormerod played a loud march that made her arms wobble and they all went back to their classrooms.

When they got there they all got their toffees and crisps and cakes out and piled them on Miss Taylor's desk.

When Josie Smith stood still and didn't bring her anything, Miss Taylor asked her, 'Have you nothing to give me or have you lost your coat now, as well as your hook?'

'I've only lost my hook,' said Josie Smith, 'and I've only got an apple.'

Miss Taylor smiled at her. 'Ah,' she said, 'you were the one with the apple. I see. Well, let's find that hook. There are two rows so there's probably a coat on the row above hanging over your name.' There was. Josie Smith hung up her coat with an apple in the pocket.

'Go and sit down,' Miss Taylor said.

Then Josie Smith remembered what Eileen had said about getting Gary Grimes and Rawley Baxter to follow her to another table. It was too late now. Everybody was sitting down and Gary Grimes and Rawley Baxter were sitting with Eileen like they always did. But when Josie Smith went to sit with them there was no room for her. Ann Lomax was in her place.

'Eileen,' whispered Josie Smith, but Eileen ignored her. Ann Lomax turned round to look at her and said, 'We don't want you sitting with us, you look like a pudding basin,' and she twirled the bangle on her wrist. Eileen twirled the bangle on her wrist and she didn't say anything. Josie Smith went away and sat in Ann Lomax's place. She wanted to cry. When drawing paper and new pencils were given out Josie Smith didn't want to draw. She wrote her name at the top and it didn't go in a straight line. She smelled dinner starting to cook and felt hungry. She wished she'd finished her breakfast.

At playtime, she stood by the railings and ate her apple and Eileen walked round holding hands with Ann Lomax.

At dinner time they had spam and mashed potatoes and baked beans. Josie Smith ate it all because she felt so hungry but then she felt sick because she was upset.

At afternoon playtime, Geoffrey Taylor ran up to her and said, 'What are you standing there like a dummy for? D'you want to play football?'

Josie Smith liked Geoffrey Taylor and she liked playing football but she wanted to wear a bangle and walk round with Eileen so she just stood there and Geoffrey Taylor ran away.

At home time she ran down the road by herself and in at her own front door.

'Mum,' she said, 'I hate school!'

'Set the table,' said Josie's mum, busy sewing, 'and don't forget to wash your hands first. Have you dirtied your new cardigan?'

'No,' said Josie Smith, 'but, Mum...'

'Set the table,' said Josie's mum.

The next day, when Eileen came to call for Josie Smith, she said, 'I'm playing with Ann Lomax at playtime and if I give her a whole packet of dolly mixtures she's going to be my best friend.'

'You haven't to bring toffees to school, Miss Potts said.'

'I've got an apple as well and the dolly mixtures'll be in my pocket and then in Ann Lomax's pocket so Miss Potts won't know unless you tell.'

'I never tell,' said Josie Smith.

At playtime, Miss Taylor, Josie's new teacher, was on duty. Everybody in the school got an apple out, except Rawley Baxter who got his plastic Batman out, and five minutes later, nearly everybody in Josie Smith's class came running to Miss Taylor, crying.

Eileen got there first.

'Mer-her! Mer-her! Mer-her!' wailed Eileen.

Josie Smith, by herself near the railings, crept a bit closer to listen.

'What's the matter?' Miss Taylor asked.

'My tooth's come out!' wailed Eileen, waving a bloodstained apple. 'Mer-her! Mer-her! Mer-her!'

'Well,' Miss Taylor said in a kind voice, 'It's all right. Just...'

Then Ann Lomax got there.

'Yar-har! Yar-har! Yar-har!' yelled Ann Lomax.

Josie Smith crept a bit closer to listen.

'What's the matter with you?' Miss Taylor asked.

'My tooth's come out!' Ann Lomax yelled, waving a bloodstained apple, 'Yar-har! Yar-har! Yar-har!'

'Well,' Miss Taylor said in a kind voice, 'It's all right. Just...'

Then Gary Grimes got there.

'Waaagh! Waaagh! Waaagh!' roared Gary Grimes.

Josie Smith stood next to Miss Taylor and listened.

'Has your tooth come out?'
Miss Taylor asked him.

'Nooo!' roared Gary Grimes, waving his
bloodstained apple. 'Two teeth! Two teeth have
come out! Waaagh! Waaagh! Waaagh!'

'Oh, for goodness' sake,' Miss Taylor said in
a not-so-kind voice, 'It's all right. Just...'

But three more crying children came, waving
their bloodstained apples, and then two more and
then four more, all roaring as loud as they could.

'Oh dear,' Miss Taylor said in a desperate
voice, 'what am I going to do?'

'It's time for the whistle,' said Josie Smith.

'Thank goodness,' Miss Taylor said, and
blew it.

In the classroom the children whose teeth
had come out stopped crying and then started

again. Some of them cried because they said it hurt. Some of them cried because they were frightened of a spot of blood. Some of them cried because they couldn't find their tooth and all the rest cried because of Eileen.

Eileen said, 'I'm getting a pound for my tooth from the tooth fairy, my mum said.'

'The tooth fairy doesn't pay a pound,' Ann Lomax said, 'she pays 50p.'

'She does not!' Geoffrey Taylor said, 'she pays 30p. I've lost both my top front teeth already, so I know. That's stupid, a pound!'

'Oh, no it's not!' Eileen said, 'Just because you haven't got a mum!'

'That's enough, Eileen!' Miss Taylor shouted, but everybody was crying and nobody could hear.

'Sit down, all of you! Will you please sit down!' shouted Miss Taylor, but everybody cried louder and nobody could hear.

Then Miss Potts marched in, banging her heels.

'What is the meaning of all this noise that I can hear from my office, Miss Taylor?'

Miss Taylor said, 'I...'

'How dare you make such a din!' roared Miss Potts. But nobody was making a din now because they were all too frightened. Even Miss Taylor looked frightened.

'Ann Lomax!' roared Miss Potts, 'What's that blood on your chin and why are you still eating an apple when playtime's over and what's all the crying about? Well?'

Ann Lomax said, 'Miss Potts, my tooth's come out and Eileen's as well and everybody else's and Eileen's lost hers and she's crying because if she doesn't find it she won't get a pound from the tooth fairy and, Miss Potts, I only get 50p and it's not fair...'

'Miss Potts, it's only 30p!'

'Miss Potts, our house hasn't got a tooth fairy!'

'Miss Potts, I've swallowed my tooth!'

'That's enough!'

Everybody was quiet.

'Josie Smith, come here,' said Miss Potts. Josie Smith went.

'Has your tooth come out?'

'No, Miss Potts.'

'No. Well your baby teeth will come out, sooner or later, but how is it that so many teeth came out today and yours didn't?'

'I don't know...' Josie Smith looked worried. Was she in trouble because her tooth hadn't come out? You can never tell when grown-ups are going to get mad at you. She pushed with her tongue at the top tooth that was a little bit loose but it didn't come out even if she pushed really hard.

'You don't know,' roared Miss Potts, 'but I know. You children who've been coming to school with toffees and chocolates and crisps and cakes – the same ones who probably eat nothing at home but fish fingers and sodden hamburgers and tinned spaghetti – *have never chewed anything in your lives*! And as soon as you bit into those apples this morning all those feeble little dangling teeth fell out. Josie Smith has never brought anything but an apple and I bet she likes meat, as well. Is that right?'

Josie Smith said, 'I like chops,' with her eyes half shut because she didn't like any other meat and always tried to take school dinner meat home. She kept a paper bag for it in her pocket and gave it to Ginger for his tea.

'Right!' shouted Miss Potts, 'Hands up all those who can't find their teeth!'

Three hands went up.

'Come here to me and bring me your apples.'

The lost teeth were found stuck in the apples except for the one that had been swallowed.

'Right! All apples into the bin!'

All the half-eaten apples went into the bin.

'Now then! I want to hear no more nonsense about the tooth fairy. The tooth fairy pays 30p! Is that understood? I said *is that understood*?'

'Yes-Miss-Potts.'

'And if anybody finds more than that under the carpet, it's been put there by their parents and when the tooth fairy sees money there she doesn't leave anything so what you get isn't fairy money at all. Now then. Some of you don't have a tooth fairy at home. Not all houses have them. My school does have a tooth fairy. In fact, she's the one who asked me to make you bring apples because there's a tooth shortage at the moment and you all know that fairies need your teeth to make furniture.'

'And cars,' a boy said.

'And cars.'

'And toys,' a girl said.

'That's enough. Those children who don't have a tooth fairy at home will leave their teeth with me in my office at home time and the tooth fairy will leave your money on my desk. 30p per tooth. Is that understood?'

'Yes–Miss–Potts.'

Gary Grimes put his hand up.

'What's the matter with you?'

'Miss Potts, two of my teeth came out and Rawley Baxter bought one for 20p.'

'Well?'

'Miss Potts, now he'll get 30p for it and I want it back.'

'Well, you can't have it back. You sold it. Another time, think on. And now every child with a tooth to look after will wrap it in a piece of paper with their name written on it and leave it on the teacher's desk. Is that understood?'

'Yes-Miss-Potts.'

'Thank you, Miss Taylor,' Miss Potts said, and she marched out, stamping her heels as she went.

When all the apples were in the bin and all the teeth lined up on the teacher's desk and everybody was sitting down, Ann Lomax was still crying.

'Now what's the matter?' Miss Taylor asked.

'Miss Taylor, Eileen won't give me the dolly mixtures she promised me just because I said she's got no tooth fairy, only her mum, and she said I was a liar and she nipped me hard on my arm and I want to go back to my own place.'

'Is that not your own place?' Miss Taylor asked. Josie Smith, watching her, thought Miss Taylor looked like Josie's mum when she had a headache and creases came in her forehead.

'No, it's not,' Ann Lomax said.

'Well whose place is it?' Miss Taylor asked.

'It's mine,' said Josie Smith.

'Change over, then,' Miss Taylor said, 'and for goodness' sake stop crying. I want to hear you all read.'

Josie Smith went back to her place but she didn't speak to Eileen all morning and Eileen didn't speak to her. In the afternoon when they had to draw a picture Eileen said, 'Will you draw me a princess?'

Josie Smith drew Eileen's picture like she always did and Eileen lent her the pink and gold from her new set of felt-tip pens.

When they were walking home, Eileen said, 'Have you got a tooth fairy at your house?'

'Yes,' said Josie Smith with her eyes a bit shut because her first tooth hadn't come out yet so she couldn't really be sure.

But that night in bed when she was whispering everything that had happened at school into Percy Panda's woolly ear, her top

70

front tooth that she had been wiggling all day, came out.

Josie Smith jumped out of bed and ran downstairs.

'What's to do, now?' asked Josie's mum, reading the paper.

'Mum!' shouted Josie Smith, 'Mum! My tooth's come out. Mum! Tell me where I have to put it for the tooth fairy!'

Josie's mum put the newspaper down and showed Josie Smith how to put the tooth under the corner of the rug in the front room.

'The hole tastes sour but it's not bleeding.'

'It'll be all right tomorrow,' said Josie's mum, looking at the gap, 'and your big tooth's showing already.'

'Mum, Miss Potts says the tooth fairy leaves 30p and she said if our house hasn't got one we can take our teeth to school.'

She waited to see if her mum would tell her to take the tooth to school but she didn't. Josie Smith went back to bed and snuggled up to Percy to get warm again.

'I hope we have got a tooth fairy,' she whispered. Then she fell asleep.

'Josie? Josie! Are you dressed? You're going to be late for school!'

Josie Smith wasn't dressed. She was in the front room in her pyjamas, looking under the rug and wishing as hard as she could that there would be 30p there.

There was 30p. But there was something else as well. There was a letter. It was the tiniest letter in the world. The envelope was smaller than Josie Smith's little finger and the writing was so tiny it was impossible to read it. Josie Smith ran in the kitchen and showed her mum. 'Is it from the tooth fairy?' she asked.

'I suppose it must be,' said Josie's mum, 'but I don't know how you're going to read it. I've never seen anything so small.'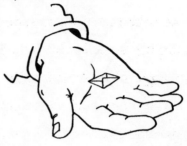

'We can ask my gran for her magnifying lens,' said Josie Smith. 'The one she uses when she can't see small print and telephone numbers. If she hasn't lost it.'

The trouble with not being able to see so well is that you can't find things, especially your glasses and your magnifying lens.

'She has lost it,' said Josie's mum, 'but I've found it. She left it behind yesterday.'

So they opened the tiniest letter in the world, addressed to Josie Smith, and it said:

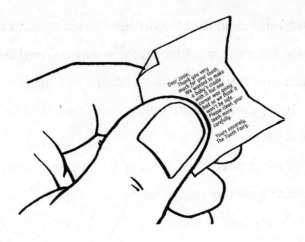

Dear Josie,
Thank you very
much for your tooth.
We wanted to make
a baby's cradle
with it but one
corner was going
bad so we think it
won't be safe.
Please clean your
teeth more
carefully.

Yours sincerely,
The Tooth Fairy.

Josie Smith told her class about it when it was News Time at school. They were all sitting on the floor round Miss Taylor and Rawley Baxter shouted out, 'That's a load of rubbish. There's no such thing as a tooth fairy and fairies don't write letters anyway!'

But Josie Smith showed them the tiny letter and Miss Taylor read it out, using Gran's magnifying glass and Rawley Baxter shut up.

The next morning, when her mum was tying her ribbon, Josie Smith said, 'Mum, I like school and I like Miss Taylor and she has her hair cut just like mine and I like Eileen, as well, because she's my best friend.'

Eileen rattled the letter box and shouted, 'Is she ready?'

'Get your coat on,' said Josie's mum, 'you're going to be late.'

Eileen rattled the letter box but Josie Smith dashed upstairs.

'I won't be long!' she shouted, 'I've got to clean my teeth!'

JOSIE SMITH
ON BONFIRE NIGHT

'Can I, Mum?' asked Josie Smith. '*Please* can I? Go on, Mum!'

'I don't know,' said Josie's mum, unfolding a piece of stuff. 'It's cold and damp and foggy and you know how you are with your chest.'

'But, Mum, I'm not ill,' said Josie Smith.

'No, and I don't want you getting ill,' said Josie's mum, 'I've enough to do as it is.'

Gary Grimes and Rawley Baxter were waiting out in the cold.

'Go on, Mum,' said Josie Smith. 'You let me go last year.'

'It wasn't weather like this last year and who's going to cross you over?'

'Jimmy Earnshaw's dad,' said Josie Smith, 'because he's helping to be in charge of the bonfire and he's taking us and looking after us all collecting wood and after dinner me and Jimmy Earnshaw are going to make a guy.'

'Jimmy Earnshaw and I,' said Josie's mum. 'If I've told you once I've told you a thousand times not to say Me and Jimmy Earnshaw and Me and Eileen.'

'Eileen's not coming,' said Josie Smith.

'No,' said Josie's mum. 'She's got more sense than to be going out in this.'

'It's because she's soft,' said Josie Smith, 'and she's frightened of dirtying her clothes.'

Gary Grimes and Rawley Baxter waited outside in the damp and Josie Smith's chest went Bam Bam Bam because she thought her mum looked as if she would say No.

'I thought you were the one who always wanted to do everything Eileen does.'

'Eileen's not coming,' Josie Smith explained again.

Josie's mum sat down and started threading up her sewing machine.

Gary Grimes and Rawley Baxter waited outside in the fog and Josie Smith's chest went Bam Bam Bam. She daren't ask again because then she'd get shouted at for pestering.

Out in the cold, damp, foggy street, Gary Grimes rattled the letter box and shouted, 'Are you coming, or not?'

'They're going without me!' wailed Josie Smith in a panic, 'and I can't go by myself or there'll be nobody to cross me over!' She started pushing her feet into her wellies that stood on the mat by the kitchen door and pulled her camouflage green anorak down from its hook. When she was halfway to the front door and halfway into her anorak, her mum shouted after her, 'Josie? Josie! Just you come back here!'

Josie Smith ran back to her mum with her chest going Bam Bam Bam.

'Fasten your coat,' said Josie's mum, 'and put that scarf on and tie it properly... and when you catch pneumonia, don't come running to me! And don't you bang that door!'

The sewing machine set off and Josie Smith set off and forgot and banged the front door.

All the streets behind Josie Smith's street were the same. Behind the last row of chimneys was a hill and on top of the hill was a tower. When it was rainy or foggy you couldn't see the tower. You couldn't see it today. You couldn't even see the hill.

Josie Smith and Gary Grimes and Rawley Baxter went down the wet, foggy street and called for Geoffrey Taylor.

'We're going collecting bommie wood,' Gary Grimes said.

'Me and my dad are, as well,' Geoffrey Taylor said. They both had their camouflage green anoraks on, just like Josie Smith's. Mr Taylor didn't say 'Don't say me and my dad'. He only winked and patted Josie Smith's fringe as they set off. Next they called for Jimmy Earnshaw and his dad and they all set off for the park.

The park was even colder than the streets. The wet leaves they trod on along the avenue smelled like mushrooms. The trees were like tall black ghosts in the fog. The bonfire was going to be in the empty field next to the swings and the park keeper had started a pile of wooden crates and cardboard boxes. Next to that was a scratched old sideboard and a sagging red armchair and a mattress with springs poking out. The park keeper told Josie Smith and Gary Grimes and Rawley Baxter and Geoffrey Taylor and Jimmy Earnshaw... and all the children from Albert Street and a lot more children Josie Smith didn't know... where to go to fetch the wood.

The big branches had to be dragged a long way from the trees that had been pruned. There were twigs clipped from the bushes and hedges to be fetched in sacks or on the wheelbarrow. Josie Smith would have liked to push the wheelbarrow but Jimmy Earnshaw and Geoffrey Taylor got it because they were the biggest and somebody gave Josie Smith a sack for twigs.

The twigs were easy to collect except that you picked up a lot of big, wet, red and yellow leaves with them. Josie Smith, being careful, tried to pick them out. Once, in Miss Valentine's class, they'd painted the red and yellow and orange leaves with candle wax. Josie Smith had taken hers home and shown them to Percy and kept them for ages and ages. She picked the really perfect ones out of the hedge clippings now and put them in her anorak pocket.

'Look sharp,' said Geoffrey Taylor's dad, coming up behind her. 'If you don't get a move on you'll have it dark.'

'It's morning, Mr Taylor,' said Josie Smith.

'It'll be dark before afternoon if this fog doesn't lift. And your mum'll have something to say if you fill your pockets with dirty leaves.'

'They're not dirty and, anyway, I'll wash them when I get home and if you put them on the window when the sun's out they're as bright as jewels. My mum said.'

'It's a wonderful season, autumn is,' said Geoffrey Taylor's dad. 'Give us your sack and I'll hold it.'

So he held Josie's sack open as she filled it with twigs.

'*Now is the time for the burning of leaves,*' said Geoffrey Taylor's dad.

'Not yet, Mr Taylor,' said Josie Smith. 'Bonfire night's on Tuesday.'

'It's a poem,' said Geoffrey Taylor's dad. And he told Josie Smith the poem and Josie Smith filled the sack and they dragged it to the bonfire between them.

When she got fed up with twigs, Josie Smith ran off the other way and chose a big branch to drag. It was a very big branch with rough wet bark and bumps that got stuck behind tufts of grass. Josie Smith pulled and heaved and heaved and pulled.

'A-her! A-her! A-her!'

And the more she pulled and heaved, the hotter and sweatier she got but she didn't give in.

She dragged and hauled and hauled and dragged.

'A-her! A-her! A-her!'

And the more she dragged and hauled, the sweatier and hotter she got but she didn't give in.

When she couldn't lift the end of the big branch any more she rolled and kicked and kicked and rolled.

'A-her! A-her! A-her!'

And the more she rolled and kicked the hotter and sweatier and completely out of breathier she got. But she didn't give in and she reached the bonfire.

'My word!' said Jimmy Earnshaw's dad, 'you're no bigger than a fourpenny rabbit but you're a good little worker all right.'

Josie Smith was so pleased that she ran off to find another big branch. She got hotter and hotter and a splinter in her finger and Mr Earnshaw took it out for her and said, 'You want to wear gloves on this job.'

'I can't,' said Josie Smith, 'because my gran made them and they've got rainbow stripes and I don't want to spoil them.'

'And haven't you an old pair?' Mr Earnshaw asked.

'I've got one... I think... ' said Josie Smith, 'but it must be in my other coat pocket.'

They stopped to go home for their dinner.

On the way home, they felt a bit tired and walked slowly along in the cold.

'Your face is as red as a beetroot,' Gary Grimes said to Josie Smith.

'Well!' said Josie Smith, 'so would yours be if you'd done any work instead of just playing with your stupid little car.' Gary Grimes didn't like work.

Halfway home Josie Smith's face stopped being red and turned white with a pale blue nose. Her woolly vest had felt hot and wet but now it felt wet and cold.

She was glad to get home where the kitchen was warm from a pie that was baking in the oven. When she'd eaten two plates of pie, Josie Smith's face turned red again and her nose began to run. She wondered if she'd caught pneumonia and she sniffed very quietly so her mum wouldn't notice. But her mum only smiled and said, 'It's because you've come in from the cold and got warm so suddenly,' and gave her a tissue. Then she said, 'You didn't feel cold in the park?'

'No,' said Josie Smith, 'I felt hot because I was working so hard.'

'And you didn't get your feet wet?'

'No, I had my wellies on. Can I go out again now?'

'All right. But if you go round with the guy when you've made it I don't want you going out of this street.'

'But, Mum, I have to go down as far as Gran's because she'll give us something for the fireworks.'

'As far as your gran's, then, and no further. And you don't go trying to buy fireworks yourselves.'

'Mum! We can't because Mr Bowker doesn't sell them to children! We have to give all the money to Jimmy Earnshaw's dad because he's buying them. Mum?'

'What's to do now? Tie that scarf properly.'

'I am tying it. Mum? Can I have some sparklers of my own to hold?'

'We'll see.'

Grown-ups always say 'We'll see' and it's worse than when they say 'No' because you can't argue. If you keep asking when they've said 'We'll see', it's pestering.

Josie Smith didn't pester. She ran out the front door and didn't bang it and she went down the wet foggy street to Jimmy Earnshaw's.

They made the guy in Jimmy Earnshaw's back yard from an old shirt and trousers, a ripped jacket, socks with holes and dirty trainers. They stuffed him full of rags and newspapers and made him a head with a balloon. Josie Smith thought of that. She was good at drawing so she drew a face on it and then they gave him a cap and sat him in Jimmy Earnshaw's pushchair from when he was small. It wasn't hard work like dragging branches and Josie Smith's vest felt wet and cold.

'Penny for the guy!' they shouted,
knocking on everybody's door.
Gary Grimes and Rawley
Baxter and Rawley Baxter's
little sister came out and
shouted, too.

'Penny for the guy!' they
shouted. Geoffrey Taylor came
out and shouted, too.

'Penny for the guy!' they
shouted. Eileen came out and said,
'I'm coming as well because my mum said I
could and I'm pushing the pram.' And they had
to let her but she soon got tired.

The afternoon got foggier and darker and
darker and foggier. Josie Smith's feet were
freezing in her wellingtons and her hands were
freezing on the pram handle as they pushed the
guy back up the street. Her gran had given them
10p and she said she was going to make parkin.

A lot of other people gave them some money to give to Mr Earnshaw for the fireworks and Mrs Earnshaw was cooking black peas.

'I'm not eating black peas,' Eileen said, 'they're dirty.'

'Don't be stupid,' Jimmy Earnshaw said. Jimmy Earnshaw had been up to Mr Bowker's shop to order the fireworks with his dad.

'There's Roman candles,' he told them, 'and Catherine wheels, and golden rain and silver rain and flower pots and rockets. I like rockets best.'

'Were there any sparklers?' asked Josie Smith. Jimmy Earnshaw didn't answer. He shouted, 'Come on! Let's push it up to Albert Street! I bet our guy's better than theirs!'

'I bet they haven't even made one!' Geoffrey Taylor said.

Jimmy Earnshaw and Geoffrey Taylor pushed the guy up to Albert Street and everybody else went in because it was so dark and spitting with rain.

'And, anyway,' Eileen said, 'I don't want to go to Albert Street because the boys are rough and you can get thumped. I'll call for you tomorrow.'

The next day, when Eileen rattled the letter box, Josie Smith was ready for school but she didn't want to go. Her head hurt and her throat hurt and her legs were tired and aching. When she went upstairs to look for her hair ribbon she wished she could get back in the cosy bed and snuggle up to Percy Panda who was still warm. Instead, she took her ribbon down and had it tied and put her coat and scarf on to walk up to school with Eileen. She couldn't tell her mum she didn't feel so well because it was bonfire night the next night and she knew what her mum would say.

'If you're not fit to go to school you're not fit to go to any bonfire.' That's what she'd say. So Josie Smith kept quiet.

In the hall, after prayers, Miss Potts started shouting about dangerous fireworks and dangerous bonfires and 'don't you dare' this and don't you dare' that and 'I'll have your parents in, is that understood? I said *is that understood*!'

'Yes-Miss-Potts.'

'There was one child, last year, who thought he could hold a Roman candle as if it were a sparkler. That child's thumb was blown right off and they never found it! And then there was a three-year-old girl who crawled inside the bonfire to help her brothers stuff newspapers in there for getting the fire going and nobody saw where she'd gone. And do you know what happened?'

'No-Miss-Potts.'

'She was still in there when they threw petrol on the bonfire and lit it and that child was burnt alive!'

Eileen began to howl. 'You're frightening me!' she screamed. 'I'm telling my mum!'

And all the infants in the front row started crying.

'That's enough!' roared Miss Potts.

One of the infants was sick all over the floor and Mr Bannister, the caretaker, came with a bucket of sand.

'I said that's enough!' roared Miss Potts in her loudest, most frightening voice. Eileen shut up. The infants stopped crying. Nobody else was sick.

Eileen said in her smarmiest voice with her head on one side, 'Miss Potts? I'm not going to the bonfire because it's dangerous.'

'Good girl,' said Miss Potts.

'Miss Potts, I'm not going either!'

'Miss Potts, I'm not, either!'

'Miss Potts, I'm not...'

'That's enough!' roared Miss Potts. 'Now you can go back to your classrooms and your teachers will tell you the story of Guy Fawkes and then you'll write about it and draw a picture. And let that be an end of it! And if any of you do go to that bonfire, you go with your parents, not on your own. I'll have no accidents happening to the children in my school! Is that understood? I said *is that understood*!'

'Yes-Miss-Potts.'

'I'm glad to hear it. Thank you, Mrs Ormerod.'

Mrs Ormerod thumped the piano till her

arms wobbled and they all went back to their classrooms.

It was a horrible day. It rained every playtime so they had to stay in. It was hot and stuffy and smelly in the classroom and Josie Smith couldn't breathe.

There was horrible meat and carrots for dinner, and rice pudding with a blob of red jam. Josie Smith didn't feel hungry and when she stirred the jam into her lumpy rice pudding to make it pink she felt sick and a dinner lady shouted at her for not eating. When it was nearly hometime she felt so horrible and hot that she lay her forehead down on the cool sheet of drawing paper where she was supposed to be drawing the Houses of Parliament and Guy Fawkes creeping towards it with a box of matches.

Eileen's voice said, 'Will you draw mine?'

Gary Grimes's voice said, 'How d'you spell "of"?'

Rawley Baxter's voice said, 'Batman!'

And then all the voices in the classroom turned into a buzzing noise that rolled about in Josie Smith's head like the sea and made her feel seasick.

'Josie? Josie!'

Josie Smith opened her eyes. Her head was still down on her paper and the drawing was going round and round. The paper was hot now so Guy Fawkes must have set fire to her drawing.

'Josie, you're ill.' Miss Taylor picked her head up.

Josie Smith wanted to say, 'I'm not ill, I can't be ill because it's bonfire night tomorrow.' But the classroom was going round and round and everything got hotter and hotter and when she opened her mouth she said, 'I want my mum...' and some tears spilled out of her eyes because she was too tired.

Josie Smith was taken home with Miss Taylor holding her hand on one side and Eileen on the other. She couldn't remember where they were going and her scarf was tied too tight but she was too tired to say so.

She felt the cool sheets and the nice woolly smell of Percy tucked in next to her.

Dr Gleeson's stethoscope was icy cold on her chest and back, and his thermometer cold in her mouth. 'That's quite a temperature she's got,' he said. 'Keep her in bed. It's bronchitis.'

Josie Smith had quite a temperature all night and the night went on for a long, long time. Josie's mum woke her up at one in the morning to hold her hot forehead in a cool hand and give her a spoonful of pink medicine.

'Give Percy some,' said Josie Smith, 'he's as hot as me.'

'It's because you've been holding him too tight,' said Josie's mum, but she gave Percy some pink medicine anyway.

'When will it be morning?' asked Josie Smith. 'I'm fed up with the night and the dark and feeling sick...'

She coughed for a bit and went back to sleep. Next time she opened her eyes, Eileen was rattling the letter box and shouting through, 'Is she ready?'

'I don't want to go to school,' said Josie Smith.

'You're not going anywhere,' said Josie's mum, and she gave her some more pink medicine.

Josie Smith stayed in bed all morning and had hot lemon and barley water and toast with a bit of honey. At one o'clock she had more pink medicine and in the afternoon Doctor Gleeson came.

'Her temperature's down,' Doctor said. 'She can get up, as long as you keep her warm.'

Josie Smith sat in the kitchen in her kilt and a jumper and a cardigan and woolly knee socks and slippers and a scarf round her throat and Percy, also wearing a scarf, on her knee. Her mum was slicing onions.

'What are you making?' asked Josie Smith.

'A hotpot,' said Josie's mum. 'I was going to take it to the bonfire supper but I might as well make it anyway. I'll tell your gran to come round.'

'But Gran's going to the bonfire with us,

Mum,' said Josie Smith. 'She's bringing parkin. She said.'

'We're not going to the bonfire,' said Josie's mum. 'You're ill. You can't go out.'

'But, Mum! I'm better now. Doctor Gleeson said. My temperature's gone down.'

Josie Smith tried so hard not to cough that the coughs squeezed into a lump in her throat and she nearly cried.

'Now don't start crying,' said Josie's mum.

'I'm not,' said Josie Smith, and she tried so hard not to cry that the lump in her throat made her cough.

'I don't want to be ill,' said Josie Smith and the cough made some tears spill over. 'I want to go to the bonfire.'

'Now, see,' said Josie's mum, 'you're ill and it can't be helped. But just because you can't go to the bonfire doesn't mean we can't have bonfire night just the same.'

'How can you have bonfire night without a bonfire?' asked Josie Smith, but she stopped coughing and crying and listened.

'Well,' said Josie's mum, 'what do you like best of all about bonfire night?'

Josie Smith thought really hard and said, 'Sparklers. I think sparklers, only I like silver rain and golden rain and flower pot fireworks as well, but sparklers I can hold myself.'

'Sparklers, then. And what next?'

'Treacle toffee... I think treacle toffee, only I like black peas in a cup as well because they're really special for bonfire night but treacle toffee tastes nicer.'

'Treacle toffee, then. And what next?'

'Jimmy Earnshaw. And Geoffrey Taylor. They said I could go with them when they take the guy down to the park because I helped with it. And Mr Earnshaw because he's kind and got my splinter out. And Mr Taylor! I bet he knows a poem about bonfire night and when he doesn't know a poem he makes one up for me!'

'And what about Eileen?'

'And Eileen because she's my best friend but she said she didn't want to go because it's dangerous.'

'Did she? Well, she can come to our bonfire night because ours won't be dangerous.'

'But will she get her clothes dirty? Because if she'll get her clothes dirty she won't come.'

'She won't get her clothes dirty,' said Josie's mum. 'She can come in her best party frock if she wants.'

'Can she?' asked Josie Smith. And then she thought and said, 'Can I put a party frock on, as well, then?'

'We've got to keep you warm,' said Josie's mum, 'but we'll see. Now, isn't there a friend you've forgotten?'

'Gary Grimes,' said Josie Smith, 'and

Rawley Baxter, as well, but I didn't want to go with them anyway because Gary Grimes didn't help to collect wood properly and Rawley Baxter always plays Batman.'

'All right,' said Josie's mum, 'but I wasn't thinking about Gary Grimes and Rawley Baxter, I was thinking about Ginger.'

'Ginger? Ginger doesn't go to the bonfire.'

'No,' said Josie's mum, 'and he'll be glad you're not going. Don't you remember last year when we came home and found him hiding under my bed? There's a lot of noise on bonfire night. He gets frightened by himself in the dark.'

'Ginger!' Josie Smith went to Ginger's basket and bent down to stroke his fur. 'It's all right, Ginger. Don't be frightened. I'm not going to the bonfire because I've got bronchitis and I had a temperature and I'm glad I'm not going now so you won't be by yourself in the dark.'

Ginger opened one eye and shut it again, purring.

'Right,' said Josie's mum, 'let me get this hotpot in the oven then I can pop across to Mrs Chadwick's for one or two things.'

'And will you tell Eileen?' said Josie Smith. 'And will you tell Mr Earnshaw and Mr Taylor or else they'll be waiting for me?'

'I'll tell Mrs Chadwick,' said Josie's mum. 'That way everybody will know.'

Josie's mum came back with a quarter of tea and half a dozen muffins and half a pound of butter and a tin of treacle.

Josie Smith and Josie's mum made treacle toffee and poured it into a tin tray. Then Josie Smith read Percy a story from her library book while her mum got on with some sewing. At the end of the story Josie Smith looked at Percy and said to her mum, 'Can Percy come to our bonfire party?'

'Of course he can,' said Josie's mum, stitching backwards and forwards and backwards and forwards, finishing a seam.

'He has no clothes,' said Josie Smith, 'nothing except my scarf.'

'Pandas don't need clothes,' said Josie's mum. 'Pandas have beautiful fur.'

'I know they have,' said Josie Smith, 'but Percy's got bronchitis.'

'All right. We'll see,' said Josie's mum. 'I've a bit of blue felt in my chest of stuff. I could make him a nice little waistcoat.'

'I'll go and look for it!' said Josie Smith.

'Stay where you are,' said Josie's mum. 'It's cold in the front. I'll go.'

So Percy was measured and his waistcoat made in less than ten minutes because Josie's mum was really fast and clever and neat at sewing. The waistcoat had two button holes and two very fancy buttons, chosen from the

button tin by Josie Smith. When
Percy had it on he looked very
dressed up and important.

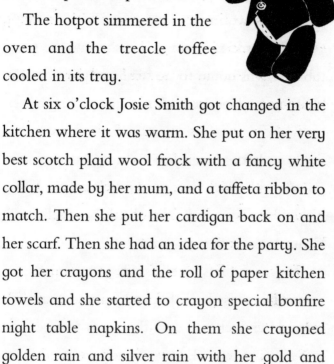

The hotpot simmered in the
oven and the treacle toffee
cooled in its tray.

At six o'clock Josie Smith got changed in the
kitchen where it was warm. She put on her very
best scotch plaid wool frock with a fancy white
collar, made by her mum, and a taffeta ribbon to
match. Then she put her cardigan back on and
her scarf. Then she had an idea for the party. She
got her crayons and the roll of paper kitchen
towels and she started to crayon special bonfire
night table napkins. On them she crayoned
golden rain and silver rain with her gold and
silver crayons and a flower pot firework going
off in the middle with all different colours. She
did a special one with a picture of a big bonfire
on it for the centre of the kitchen table.

'That's good,' said Josie's mum, 'it'll keep the hotpot warm for us. Here's your gran coming in.'

Josie's gran came in with a paper bag full of parkin still warm from her oven.

'My word!' she said, when she saw the party table, 'I was going to go to the bonfire but I'm glad I came here instead. Are you feeling better, love?'

'I am better,' said Josie Smith, 'but we can't go to the bonfire because Ginger would be by himself in the dark and he'd be frightened. Gran, look at Percy's waistcoat!'

'My goodness me!' said Josie's gran, 'I remember those brass buttons from your mum's navy blue jacket... and that was before you were born. Here's Eileen coming in.'

Eileen came in and said, 'What's all those drawings on the table for? I've brought us a packet of sparklers each and my dad's coming after with some fireworks. He's having his tea now. And my mum said I can stay to my tea here because I've got a cough as well, anyway.'

Eileen was wearing her best frock and black patent shoes with ankle straps. Josie Smith in her slippers wished she had shoes with ankle straps but then she forgot because she was hungry.

'Is it ready?' she said, 'I'm starving, Mum.'

'You *are* feeling better,' said Josie's mum and she started serving the hotpot while Josie Smith crayoned another special bonfire night napkin for Eileen.

'Can I have one without crayoning on it, as well?' asked Eileen, 'So I don't need to dirty this one and then I can take it home?'

'You do as you please,' said Josie's mum. 'Pass your plate. Is that Mrs Earnshaw?'

'I've brought you some black peas,' Mrs Earnshaw said. 'Just a little pan full and some paper cups. I heard your Josie's not so well. I'm on my way to the bonfire but I wish I were staying with you. It's that dark and wet out.'

Josie Smith ate black peas and a buttered muffin and lots of toasty browned potatoes from the top of the hotpot. Under the table, Ginger waited for the meat Josie Smith didn't want. Eileen ate her black peas because Josie Smith ate them. She didn't say they were dirty.

'Let's clear the table,' said Josie's mum, 'and have treacle toffee and parkin. Here's your dad coming in, Eileen.'

'I've brought a couple of fireworks,' said Eileen's dad. 'There wasn't much left by this afternoon. I'll let them off in the yard.'

But first he had to help with the treacle toffee because Josie's mum tried and Josie's gran tried and Josie Smith and Eileen tried together but the treacle toffee was hard as rock and nobody could break it. Eileen's dad decided to use a hammer. He had to go next door for it and when he came back Eileen's mum was with him and they all ate a piece of parkin.

'I like parkin best of all,' said Eileen with her mouth full.

'Eileen,' said Eileen's mum, 'don't talk with your mouth full. Here's Mr Earnshaw and Jimmy coming in.'

'It's raining cats and dogs,' Mr Earnshaw said, 'so we all came away. I've brought a few fireworks for your Josie. I heard she wasn't so well.'

Jimmy Earnshaw sat down next to Josie Smith. 'My dad said you worked so hard collecting bommie wood that you should have the fireworks that were left.'

Josie Smith's eyes were shining because Jimmy Earnshaw was sitting next to her. She liked having the fireworks as well.

'Did the bonfire not get going?' she asked him, 'because it was raining hard?'

''Course it did,' Jimmy Earnshaw said. 'It started raining after. And you should have seen the guy. That was a dead good idea you had, a head made out of a balloon. You should have heard it bang!'

Josie Smith's eyes shone even more because he liked her good idea. She gave him a piece of parkin. Jimmy Earnshaw told her every single thing about the bonfire, how they had trouble lighting it, how his dad had got it going and how it went out again and his dad got it going again and what Geoffrey Taylor said and what Geoffrey Taylor's dad said and what the children from Albert Street said and how one of them stole some fireworks.

Josie Smith gave him a piece of treacle toffee.

'It's hard,' he said, trying to bite it.

'You have to suck it,' said Josie Smith, 'then it sticks your teeth together. Mum! Here's Mr Taylor.'

Mr Taylor and Geoffrey Taylor came in with four packets of sparklers.

'Do I smell hotpot?' Mr Taylor asked.

'Wasn't there some at the bonfire?' asked Josie's mum.

'Four big dishes,' Mr Taylor said, 'but I was helping to get the fire going and then lighting fireworks and what with it starting raining...'

'Sit down,' said Josie's mum. 'You, too, Geoffrey, come on.'

There weren't enough chairs and some had to be brought from the front room but there was enough hotpot and parkin and black peas and treacle toffee and plenty of fireworks. Mr Taylor and Mr Earnshaw let them off in the yard once it stopped raining and they switched off the light in the kitchen.

There were flowerpots and Roman candles and silver rain and golden rain and Catherine wheels, nailed to the shed door, that wouldn't set off for ages, and rockets that lit up the smoky sky. They all cried 'Eeeeh!' and 'Oooh!' and 'Aaagh!' Percy, with his fat tummy buttoned into his waistcoat, and Ginger, with his fat tummy full of hotpot, sat at the window and watched, too.

Then they lit their sparklers.

'I'm writing my name!' shouted Josie Smith, writing 'Josie' in the dark.

'I don't want one!' Eileen cried, 'I'm frightened of burning my hand.'

'It's all right, Eileen,' said Josie Smith. 'Look! Hold it straight out like me.'

But Eileen wouldn't hold it, so Josie Smith wrote 'Eileen' in the dark for her.

Then Gary Grimes and Rawley Baxter came rattling at the letter box and shouting, 'Can we come to your fireworks party?' because they could see the fireworks going off over the wall of Josie Smith's yard. So they came in, too.

'I should have baked a few potatoes...' said Josie's mum.

Geoffrey Taylor and Geoffrey Taylor's dad had finished all the hotpot and all that was left of the peas and parkin was an empty pan and some crumbs. But there were still some sparklers and still two sky rockets and more chunks of treacle toffee to stick their teeth together and the grown-ups had cups of tea. The party went on past bedtime.

When Josie Smith got into bed and her mum gave her some pink medicine and hung Percy's waistcoat on the bedpost, Josie Smith said, 'That was the best bonfire night we've ever had, wasn't it, Mum?'

'I think it was,' said Josie's mum.

And everybody else thought so too. Especially – upside down in his basket, paws in the air and tummy bulging with hotpot – Ginger.

Make friends with Josie Smith

JOSIE SMITH IN WINTER
By Magdalen Nabb
Illustrated by Karen Donnelly

Winter brings worries for Josie Smith.
Will Ginger get lost, out in the howling wind?
Will it ever snow? And will Mum's flu get better?
Find out how Josie Smith ends up having a
wonderful time in winter!

Collins
An imprint of HarperCollins*Publishers*

Make friends with Josie Smith

JOSIE SMITH IN SPRING
By Magdalen Nabb
Illustrated by Karen Donnelly

Spring brings surprises for Josie Smith!
She finds out that you can plant seeds
if you invent a garden.
That your mum can make you steal
something by accident.
And that there's more than
one kind of Easter egg.

Collins
An imprint of HarperCollins*Publishers*

Make friends with Josie Smith

JOSIE SMITH IN SUMMER
By Magdalen Nabb
Illustrated by Karen Donnelly

Summer – and magic is in the air for Josie Smith.
She goes swimming in her back yard.
She hears about a fish who turned into a little girl.
And, when she needs it most, a magical
voice helps her out.

Collins
An imprint of HarperCollinsPublishers

Order Form

To order direct from the publishers, just make a list of the titles you want and fill in the form below:

Name ....

Address ....

....

....

Send to: Dept 6, HarperCollins Publishers Ltd, Westerhill Road, Bishopbriggs, Glasgow G64 2QT.

Please enclose a cheque or postal order to the value of the cover price, plus:

UK & BFPO: Add £1.00 for the first book, and 25p per copy for each additional book ordered.

Overseas and Eire: Add £2.95 service charge. Books will be sent by surface mail but quotes for airmail despatch will be given on request.

A 24-hour telephone ordering service is available to holders of Visa, MasterCard, Amex or Switch cards on 0141- 772 2281.

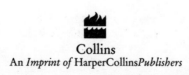

Collins
An *Imprint of* HarperCollins*Publishers*